JACK RUSSELL: Dog Detective

The Phantom Mudder

DARREL & SALLY ODGERS

D0596797

SCHOLASTIC CANADA LTD.

New York   Toronto   London   Auckland   Sydney
Mexico City   New Delhi   Hong Kong   Buenos Aires

Scholastic Canada Ltd.
604 King Street West, Toronto, Ontario M5V 1E1, Canada

Scholastic Inc.
557 Broadway, New York, NY 10012, USA

Scholastic Australia Pty Limited
PO Box 579, Gosford, NSW 2250, Australia

Scholastic New Zealand Limited
Private Bag 94407, Greenmount, Auckland, New Zealand

Scholastic Children's Books
Euston House, 24 Eversholt Street,
London NW1 1DB, UK

Library and Archives Canada Cataloguing in Publication

Odgers, Darrel
The phantom mudder / Darrel & Sally Odgers ; Janine Dawson, illustrator
(Jack Russell, dog detective ; 2)
ISBN 0-439-93801-5

I. Odgers, Sally, 1957- II. Dawson, Janine III. Title. IV. Series: Odgers,
Darrel.
Jack Russell, dog detective ; 2.

PZ7.O2374Ph 2006   j823'.92   C2006-902683-1

6 5 4 3 2 1   Printed in Canada   06 07 08 09 10

Dear Readers,

The book *you've* just started to read is about me and my friends and how we solved the case of the Phantom Mudder. To save time, I'll introduce all of us to you now. Of course, if you know us already, you can skip ahead to Chapter One.

I am Jack Russell, Dog Detective. I live with my landlord, Sarge, in Doggeroo. Sarge detects human-type crimes. I detect important crimes. Those are the ones that deal with dogs! I'm a Jack Russell terrier, so I am dogged and intelligent.

Next door to Sarge and me live Auntie Tidge and Foxy. Auntie Tidge is wonderful. She has dog biscuits. Foxy is not so wonderful. He's a fox terrier (more or less). He used to be a street dog and a thief, but he's reformed now. Auntie Tidge has even gotten rid of his fleas. Foxy sometimes helps me with my cases.

Uptown Lord Setter (Lord Red for short) lives in Uptown House with Caterina Smith. Lord Red means well. He tries to help with my cases, but he sometimes gets overexcited.

That's all you need to know, so let's start Chapter One.

Yours doggedly,

Jack Russell—the detective with a nose for crime

Mud

One wet Friday, Sarge told me about the Doggeroo Dog Show.

"It's been held for a hundred and fifty years, Jack," Sarge said. "It's one of the oldest dog shows around."

I wagged my tail. I like to please Sarge.

"I'm working there as a **steward**," said Sarge. "What do you think, Jack? Want to go to a dog show tomorrow?"

I snorted. That's what I think of dog shows.

"Great," said Sarge. "You can come."

Jack's Facts

Dogs understand what humans say.
Humans think they understand what
dogs say.
Therefore, dogs are smarter than humans.
This is a fact.

That afternoon, Foxy and I dug a big hole near the apple tree.

Most dogs won't let another dog help bury a bone, but I'm not like that.

I know, and Foxy knows, that my garden is my **terrier-tory**. That means no dog can come into the garden without my permission.

"It's very muddy, Jack," said Foxy, when we finished the hole. "I've got mud all over my paws."

"Who cares?" I dropped the bone into the hole and started to push the mud on top of it with my nose. "Mud's good."

"Foxy! Foxy Woxy!" Auntie Tidge was calling Foxy home.

I laughed. "I bet she wants to give you a bath."

"Auntie Tidge would never **terrier-ize** me that way," said Foxy. "She will just wipe the mud off my paws."

"Foxy Woxy!"

"Coming!" Foxy yapped, and took off through the hedge.

I walked over the spot where we buried my bone to firm down the mud. While I did that, I made a quick **nose map**.

Jack's Map

1. Mud everywhere.

2. The buried beef bone.

3. A place under the tree where a cat sat last Thursday.

I waited a while. *Sniff-sniff.* Then I smelled the smell I expected to smell.

4. Flowery soap and wet dog.

I heard Foxy's voice faintly howling, "I'll get you for this, Jack Russell!"

Told you so, I thought.

"Jackie Wackie?" That was Auntie Tidge calling me. I love Auntie Tidge, so I crawled through the hedge and raced around the corner, wagging my tail.

"How's my dear Jack?" Auntie Tidge

asked as she bent down to pet me.

I **Jack-jumped** up and knocked her glasses sideways so I could give her a big lick on the nose. She loves it when I do that.

Auntie Tidge caught me. "Bath time, Jack," said Auntie Tidge.

Traitor.

Jack's Glossary

Steward. *Person at a dog show who sees that the rules and schedule are followed.*

Terrier-tory. *The ground or land claimed by a terrier.*

Terrier-ize. *Frighten.*

Nose map. *Way of storing information collected by the nose.*

Jack-jump. *A sudden jump by a Jack.*

Smelling Soap

The next morning, we went to the show with Sarge and Auntie Tidge.

I stuck my head out the car window.

<u>Jack's Facts</u>

Dogs have noses. Cars have windows. One must be stuck out the other. This is a fact.

I sneezed. "Everything smells like soap," I complained to Foxy.

"*You* smell like soap, Jack Russell," growled Foxy.

Outside Doggeroo Hall, it was wet and muddy. Auntie Tidge carried us inside. "You go and play, darlings, while I find my friend Dora," said Auntie Tidge.

The dogs inside the hall all smelled like soap, especially Lord Red, who lives at Uptown House with Caterina Smith. He was racing in circles, whirling his tail.

He didn't even notice Foxy and me.

"Lordie, *Lordie!*" called Caterina Smith. "Are your paws muddy?"

Red ran faster.

"There's that stupid setter running loose again," said a man with three chihuahuas on leashes. "It shouldn't be allowed."

"The steward tried to ban *my* dog last year for bad behavior," said a man with gray mud on his boots. He was holding a poodle wearing a muzzle. "He should have banned the setter."

"Your dog bit the judge's wife," the three-chihuahuas man pointed out.

"She got in the way. That setter is about to—watch out!"

There was a scream from over near the door.

Lord Red had **greeted** a woman who was wearing high-heeled shoes.

"Lordie, *Lordie*, come here!" called Caterina Smith. She pulled Red away.

High Heels stamped her foot. Red yelped and tucked his tail between his legs.

"Oops," said High Heels. "I must have stepped on his tail."

"Let me wipe off your coat," said Caterina Smith. "A little soap will fix it."

High Heels pushed her away. "Never mind. Dogs will be dogs."

"Lord Red gets so excited," said Caterina Smith. "I hope your coat will be all right."

"What's a bit of mud on a brand-new coat?" said High Heels. "At the show last week a spaniel chewed the heels right off my new shoes, and the week before, a bulldog ate my gold lipstick. And last year in this very hall I was—"

"Did it make the bulldog sick?" interrupted Caterina Smith.

"What? Oh, no. The *bulldog* was just fine."

"That's the main thing, isn't it?" said Caterina Smith. "Oops!" she added as Red tried to greet the woman again. "Better go!" She led Red away.

High Heels stared after them. Then she marched off. Foxy and I jumped out of her way just in time, and one of the chihuahuas growled at us.

"I see terrier toothpicks."

Foxy and I didn't want to be forced to hurt the chihuahua, so we left.

There were dogs everywhere. The

three **squekes** that live on the corner were yipping, doing what squekes do.

Shuffle, the pug that lives near the park, was sulking in his basket. "I don't like dog shows," he snuffled crossly.

Polly, the dachshund from across the river, was **daching** around with her person, Gloria Smote. Jill Russell, who lives near the train station, was guarding a bone in the corner. Jill always pokes me with her nose. She's a real **ace**!

Jack's Facts

Jack is a male name.
Jill is a female name.
Therefore, a female Jack Russell is really a
Jill Russell.
This is a fact.

All these dogs smelled of soap. I sneezed.

<u>Jack's Glossary</u>

Greet. *This is done by rising to the hind legs and clutching a person with the paws while slurping them up the face.*

Squekes. *Small hairy dogs with bulging eyes and loud yips.*

Daching. *The way dachshunds move around.*

Ace. *Great, fine, the very best.*

15

Suspecting Skullduggery

I was still sneezing when Lord Red raced up.

"Jack! Jack!" he barked. His whirling tail sent two shih tzus scampering. "What's going down, Jack?"

"You're racing around, scaring shih tzus," I said.

"Who's being **dognapped**? Who's stealing balls? Who's doing bad things?"

Ever since I solved the case of the Doggeroo Dog Den, Lord Red has been hoping I'll let him help me detect something.

"You're the one doing bad things," I said. "Why did you greet that High Heels woman?"

"Because she came with the dog biscuit man," said Red. "I like the dog biscuit man. Caterina Smith says he might give me a ribbon."

Foxy pricked up his ears. "What dog biscuit man? Where?" (Foxy loves dog biscuits.)

"The dog biscuit man is the judge," said Red. "He smells of dog biscuits. My tail hurts, Jack. Do you think I can win a ribbon with a sore tail? Will you investigate, Jack?"

"Don't be silly," I said. "I investigate **skulldoggery**, not sore tails."

Red got low to the ground and stuck his tail in the air. "If I see any skulldoggery, can I come and tell you, Jack?"

"Of course," I said. "Jack Russell's the name, detection's the game."

Red was really pleased.

"Lordie, *Lordie*!"

"Caterina Smith is calling," said Red. "See you later, Jack." He trotted off.

Foxy sniffed the air. "I'm going to find Auntie Tidge and get a **special biscuit.**"

After Foxy had gone, I looked for Sarge. On the way, I saw High Heels. She had a smeary wet patch on her coat. She was talking to the man who smelled of dog biscuits.

"Are you enjoying this show, Kate?" asked Biscuits.

"Oh, yes," said High Heels. "All these

lovely, clean, shiny dogs . . ."

Biscuits smiled and patted her on the shoulder.

". . . although one *did* get mud all over my new coat," she continued.

"I expect it was that setter of Caterina Smith's," said Biscuits. "He's a friendly dog, and completely harmless."

"A friendly dog!" agreed the woman. "Could you give me a show schedule, dear? I like to know which group comes next."

"Here you are, dear." Biscuits took a schedule out of his pocket and gave it to her.

High Heels clicked her fingers at me. "Who's a sweet little doggy?"

I sniffed and walked away. I was offended.

Jack's Facts

A Jack Russell may be sweet.
A Jack Russell may be little.
A Jack Russell is never a "sweet little doggy."
This is a fact.

Just then, I saw the three-chihuahuas
man again. He was talking to Sarge in a
loud, rough voice.

"Now, look here!" he said.

Immediately, I suspected skulldoggery.

"No, *you* look here, Mr. Latiman," said Sarge. "You can't show those dogs today."

"And why not?" Mr. Latiman moved a step closer.

"Back off," I growled. My hackles rose. This looked like a case for Jack Russell, Dog Detective!

"Entries closed two weeks ago," said Sarge. "Rules are rules. Take your dogs home, Mr. Latiman."

Mr. Latiman snarled. "You'll be sorry you took this attitude, Sergeant Russell!"

I growled to show the man that Sarge was protected by a capable **doggyguard**.

"Back off, Jack," rumbled one of the

21

chihuahuas. "You smell like soap."

I didn't want to be forced to hurt the chihuahua, so I went back to Foxy and Auntie Tidge. The smell of soap and shampoo and Pooch Polish and chew toys and wet dog and mud was getting stronger every minute.

Lord Red bounded up. "Jack, Jack, I've found some skulldoggery! Will you investigate, Jack?"

"That depends," I said. "What kind of skulldoggery?"

"Someone has **muddied** Shuffle the pug," barked Red. "Shuffle the pug was clean. Now he is all muddied. Isn't that skulldoggery, Jack?"

"No," I said. "That's just natural."

Jack's Glossary

Dognap. *The same as kidnap, only concerns a dog instead of a kid.*

Skulldoggery. *Bad goings-on that concern dogs.*

Special biscuits. *Auntie Tidge makes these. They don't harm terrier teeth.*

Doggyguard. *A bodyguard that is a dog.*

Muddied. *Being covered or splattered with mud.*

Soggy Doggy

"Welcome to the one-hundred-and-fiftieth Doggeroo Dog Show!" howled a **loudhowler.** "A special welcome to Judge Gibbs and to our new steward, Sergeant Russell."

No one took any notice, so the loudhowler howled it again, louder. Lots of dogs howled back.

Jack's Facts

When a howler howls, polite dogs howl back.
This is a fact.

"First class—spaniels!" howled the loudhowler.

"What a pity it's so muddy today," Auntie Tidge said to Dora Barkins as the spaniels entered the ring. The man who smelled of dog biscuits was waiting for them in the center. "That pug looks as if he's been rolling in mud," said Dora, staring at Shuffle.

The spaniels were walking in circles around Judge Gibbs while Sarge ticked off numbers on his clipboard. Soon the judge tied a ribbon on one of the collars.

"Second class—dachshunds," howled the loudhowler as the spaniels left the ring.

The dachshunds dached toward the ring and began to trot around in circles.

I was surprised to see that Polly wasn't with them.

"Where's Polly?" I wondered aloud to Foxy.

"Maybe she's been **dognapped**," suggested Foxy.

"In that case," I said, "I'll need to investigate."

Foxy sniffed and pricked his ears. "I smell dog biscuits. Do you hear a biscuit bag, Jack?"

Just then, Gloria Smote rushed up with Polly on a leash. Polly was dripping all over the place. She was a very soggy doggy.

"Why is your dog wet, Gloria?" asked Sarge.

"I washed her," explained Gloria Smote.

"You should have washed her earlier,"

said Sarge. "You can't show a wet dog."

Gloria's eyes looked as red as a white rabbit's. "I did wash her earlier. Just before her class was called I found her covered in mud. I had to wash her again."

"Rules are rules," Sarge said. "You can't show Polly in the dachshund class, Gloria. Tell you what. Why not transfer her entry to the small-dog class?"

Gloria smiled. She has little white teeth just like Polly's. "Oh, Sergeant Russell, you are smart! I'll go and dry her now."

I decided I like Gloria Smote.

Foxy and I went to help by licking Polly dry. Polly smelled of soap and dog biscuits.

"Stop that!" said Gloria Smote. "I don't want dog slobber all over Polly!"

I decided I don't like Gloria Smote.

As Foxy and I retreated, Lord Red dashed up, whirring his tail. "Jack, Jack! I've found some more skulldoggery!"

"What is it this time, Red?" I asked.

"Somebody muddied Polly!" said Red. "That's skulldoggery, isn't it?"

I was about to remind Red that mud was not skulldoggery, when I thought again. If someone had muddied Shuffle *and* Polly, maybe there really *was* skulldoggery afoot.

I couldn't investigate the case right away, because Muddy Boots and his poodle were bullying Sarge. This called for Sarge's doggyguard—me.

I snarled.

The poodle growled.

Muddy Boots kicked me away. "Give

me a number, Steward! I'm going to show my dog. I paid my entry fee two weeks ago."

"And I paid it back," said Sarge. "You were banned from the last show, Mr. Bootle. You are not allowed to show that dog. It bites."

"I was framed!" snapped Muddy Boots. "It wasn't my fault my dog bit that woman! Some dogs bite. What can you do?"

"Rules are rules," said Sarge.

Muddy Boots sneered. "You made an exception for that dripping dachshund."

"That's different," said Sarge. "You can't show your dog today, Mr. Bootle. And don't come next year, either."

Muddy Boots pointed at Sarge. "You'll be sorry you said that!"

"I doubt it," said Sarge. "And don't you ever kick my dog again!" He bent to rub my ears. "Okay, Jack?"

"Third class–dalmatians!" howled the loudhowler.

Five black dogs came toward us, led by angry people.

"No, no," said Sarge. "This is the dalmatian class, not the black Labrador class."

"We *are* the dalmatian class!" snapped one woman.

Sarge frowned. "Surely dalmatians have spots, don't they?"

"They *do* have spots!" said a man. "Someone's covered our dogs with mud."

We looked. I sniffed. I could smell mud, and soap, and . . . something else. I sneezed. My superior **super-sniffer** still wasn't working very well.

"You can't show muddy dogs," said Sarge.

The loudhowler called the schnauzer class instead.

Four people came up with schnauzers. Sarge ticked them off on his clipboard. "Where are the other two?" he asked. "I have six entries listed here."

"Here," said Mr. Crisp. "Someone's gotten mud all over my dogs! Just *look* at them!"

Sarge and I looked at the muddied schnauzers.

"This is getting ridiculous!" said Sarge. "Go and wash them." He borrowed the loudhowler. "Attention, everyone! *Please* control your dogs! Muddy dogs may *not* be shown!"

Mr. Crisp went away, and the rest of the class trotted into the ring.

Lord Red came bounding up. "Are you going to investigate, Jack? Are you?"

"Yes," I said. "Jack Russell's the name, detection's the game. I already have some suspects."

Jack's Glossary

Loudhowler. *A thing dog shows have so people and dogs can hear instructions.*

Super-sniffer. *Jack's nose in super-tracking mode.*

The Phantom Mudder Strikes Again

"What can I do, Jack?" Lord Red asked as he pranced around.

"Find out how many dogs have been muddied," I said.

Red ran off, and I heard him barking out questions. I trotted off to interview my first suspect.

Polly was sitting in a cage with a blanket over the top. I poked my superior super-sniffer through the folds. I sniffed. I could still smell soap, but when I got closer, I could also detect damp dog and dog biscuit and Foxy slobber.

Polly glared at me. "Go away, Jack Russell. Gloria Smote will be angry if you lick my face again."

"It isn't *my* fault you got muddied!" I said. I looked at her sternly. "Come clean, Polly. Why did you do it? Why did you muddy yourself up before your class?"

Polly sniffed. "Why would I do a thing like that, Jack Russell?"

"Because you hate shows," I said.

"I like shows," said Polly. "If I win a ribbon, Gloria Smote is pleased. I like to please Gloria Smote."

Jack's Facts

Dogs don't do anything if there's nothing in it for them.
People sometimes do.
That makes dogs smarter than people.
This is a fact.

"How did you get muddied, then?" I demanded.

"I don't know," said Polly. "I didn't see."

"You must have smelled whoever it was. Dachs might not have superior super-sniffers like Jacks, but they can still sniff."

"A dach can sniff as well as any Jack," snapped Polly. "Tell me, Jack Russell. What can *your* superior super-sniffer sniff today?"

I *sniff-sniffed* as I tried to make a nose map.

Jack's Map

1. Dog and soap.

2. People and soap.

3. Biscuits and soap.

4. Mud and soap.

5. Soap.

"I see what you mean," I said. "The crime scene is contaminated by soap."

I went to interview more suspects. The muddied dalmatians and the muddied schnauzers all told the same story. Shuffle the pug admitted that he hated shows, but he denied muddying himself in protest. His evidence agreed with Polly's. Someone had put mud on him, but he hadn't noticed who. *Hmm*, I thought. These dogs are not **pup-etrators.** These dogs are the victims of a Phantom Mudder.

The schnauzer class finished, and the loudhowler howled that the setters would be judged after the squekes.

"Lordie? *Lordie?*" Caterina Smith was calling Lord Red.

I'd sent Red to count muddied dogs, but I'd already interviewed most of the victims. Where was Red?

Foxy was sitting under Auntie Tidge's chair, eating a special biscuit. "Hey, Foxy," I said. "Have you seen Red?"

"No," said Foxy. "I did see a black setter, though."

"Are you sure?"

Foxy licked his whiskers. "Hard to be

sure of anything with all this soap around."

Foxy was right. I was having a **terrier-ble** time detecting without the full use of my superior super-sniffer.

"There he goes again!" said Foxy as a big black dog raced by.

"Jack—*Jack!*" barked the black setter. Then I knew it wasn't a black setter. It was Red.

The Phantom Mudder had struck again, and this time Red was the victim.

Jack's Facts

Even superior super-sniffers become less reliable when affected by soap.
This is a fact.

Jack's Glossary

Pup-etrators. *Perpetrators (another word for criminals) who happen to be pups or dogs.*

Terrier-ble. *Not good — especially for a dog*

 ## Was Red Doggled?

"Jack, Jack! I found eight muddied dogs!" Red wagged his tail, splattering me with mud. "Oops, make that nine!" sputtered Red.

"Ten," I said, glaring at Red.

"Eleven!" said Red as a squeke yipped by. It looked as if it had been dipped in melted chocolate. "Dora Barkins won't be happy with that squeke," said Red. "Muddied squekes can't win ribbons, and the squeke class is soon."

I didn't point out that muddied setters couldn't win ribbons, either. I

didn't want to lead the witness.

"Do you know who muddied you?" I asked.

"Of course," said Red.

"You *do*?" Maybe Red wasn't as thick between the ears as I'd always thought.

"Of course I know," said Red.

"Who?" I asked doggedly. (You have to be dogged to get much sense out of Red.)

"The Phantom Mudder muddied me. Who else?"

I groaned.

With my lead witness a washout (and needing a wash), I tracked down a new line of inquiry.

Dog shows are about dogs, but the dogs weren't doing the muddying.

Dog shows are also about people.

Think, Jack, I told myself. *Why would a person become a Phantom Mudder?*

What if someone wanted his dog to win and **doggled** the competition by muddying competing dogs? But that would only make sense if just one class had been doggled.

Someone with a dachshund might doggle Polly so his own dachshund could win. But no one would show a dachshund, a schnauzer, a dalmatian, a pug, a squeke, *and* a setter.

Besides, *all* the dalmatians had been muddied, so the whole class had been canceled. What was the use of doggling them?

"Stand still," I said to Red. I called upon my superior super-sniffer.

"What do you sniff, Jack?" asked Red.

"Shush," I said. "I'm making a nose map."

It didn't take long for me to nose-map Red.

Jack's Map

1. Soap and mud.

2. Soap, mud, and Pooch Polish.

3. Soap, mud, and more soap.

4. Soap, mud, and dog biscuit.

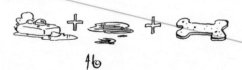

"Did someone give you a dog biscuit today?" I asked Red.

Red looked shifty. "Caterina Smith says people at dog shows aren't allowed to give dogs biscuits."

I hoped Auntie Tidge didn't know that. She'd brought special biscuits for Foxy and me. "Why?"

"In case someone gets doggled by a biscuit with sleepy stuff in it."

I sniffed Red's face again. There was that faint hint of dog biscuit. It smelled like special biscuit.

Pause for thought. *Could Auntie Tidge be the Phantom Mudder?*

Dogwash! "Red," I said, "you're lying. Someone *did* give you a dog biscuit today. Who was it?"

Red looked embarrassed. "Nobody. I

mean, I only sort of found some."

"And did you sort of eat them?"

"Sort of," admitted Red. He put his
nose down by mine. "A doggler would
doggle the dog he wanted to doggle. He
wouldn't leave doggled biscuits lying
around for just any dog to eat."

"I'm not so sure," I said.

"Anyway, I wasn't doggled," said Red
cheerfully. "I was only muddied." He
cocked his head. "Caterina Smith is
calling."

Red raced off, startling the muddied
squeke as he went. Red was certain he
hadn't been doggled.

I was certain he had.

I went back to Polly.

"Go away, Jack Russell," said Gloria
Smote. "I don't want Jack-lick on Polly."

I decided I *really* don't like Gloria Smote.

"Polly, have you eaten a dog biscuit today?" I asked.

Polly licked her chops. "I'm not allowed to accept biscuits at dog shows."

"Thanks," I said to Polly. "That's all I need to know."

<u>Jack's Facts</u>

Finding biscuits is not the same thing as accepting biscuits.
It is also not the same thing as stealing biscuits.
Anything left in reach of a dog is that dog's by right.
This should be a fact.

I asked a dalmatian and one of the muddied schnauzers the same question I'd asked Red and Polly. I got the same result.

They said they had not accepted any dog biscuits from anyone today.

Neither of them actually said they hadn't *eaten* any dog biscuits. And when I pressed them, they admitted they had sort of found some dog biscuits. And sort of eaten them.

I knew in my bones that I was on the right track. I'd established the means of the crime. The Phantom Mudder was tempting dogs with biscuits, then muddying them while they ate.

That was the means. What about opportunity and motive?

Jack's Glossary

Doggled. *Like hobbling a racehorse by doing something that will stop it from winning a race, but done to a dog.*

# Foxy Foxes the Judge

I *sniff-sniffed* around. I tracked down places where dog biscuits had been. I also discovered other muddied dogs.

The Phantom Mudder had struck again and again.

I *sniff-sniffed* some more, and then I remembered something.

Judge Gibbs smelled of dog biscuits. Red called him "the dog biscuit man."

Maybe Judge Gibbs was the Phantom Mudder? He had the means. He had the biscuits.

"Why would Judge Gibbs muddy a dog?" asked Foxy when I told him my new theory. "Why would he muddy dogs he's supposed to judge?"

"Maybe he likes small classes," I said. As I spoke, Judge Gibbs was judging five squekes. Three other entries had been muddied.

"But he wouldn't rather judge *no* class," snapped Foxy. "Remember the dalmatians."

"**Bathwater!**" I said. "Those dalmatians ruin my theory."

"Maybe Judge Gibbs just doesn't like dalmatians," said Foxy.

"I wonder if Judge Gibbs likes fox terriers," I suggested. "You go and **fox** him, Foxy. Pretend to be a very nice dog. See if he muddies you."

"Why should I?" asked Foxy.

"He might give you a dog biscuit," I said. "If he does, bring it to me for **paw-rensic testing.**"

Foxy is anyone's for a dog biscuit, so he trotted off to fox Judge Gibbs, who had just finished tying a ribbon on a squeke. I watched from behind a box of Pooch Polish.

Jack's Facts

Pooch Polish is like soap.
Therefore, Pooch Polish should never be
used on a dog.
However, it is good to hide behind.
This is a fact.

Foxy began to fox Judge Gibbs. He
pretended to be a very nice dog. He
wagged his tail.

The judge bent and rubbed Foxy's
ears. "Where did you spring from, Foxy?"

Foxy got up on his hind paws and
sniffed Judge Gibbs's pocket. "Jack sent me
to fox you," he yipped.

Judge Gibbs laughed. "Can you smell
dog biscuits? I shouldn't give you one, you
know. Not without asking your owner."

Sniff-sniff, went Foxy. He scraped Judge Gibbs's leg with one paw and whined. Then he did the **paw thing**. That was just the way I would have acted the part of a greedy dog. Only Foxy wasn't acting.

"Just one, then," said Judge Gibbs. "No more."

He took a special biscuit out of his pocket and gave it to Foxy. "Off you go, Foxy. It's almost time for me to judge the setter class."

I watched Foxy take the special biscuit in his jaws. I stared at Judge Gibbs. Would he muddy Foxy? No, he just judged the setters.

Red wasn't with them. He was still being bathed by Caterina Smith.

Foxy came back to me. "Why are you

hiding behind the Pooch Polish box, Jack?"

"I was lying in wait while you foxed Judge Gibbs," I said. "Where is that dog biscuit he gave you?"

"I ate it," said Foxy.

"I told you I wanted it for paw-rensic testing!"

"Well, I did some **jaw-rensic testing**," said Foxy. "It wasn't doggled."

Foxy was right. The judge hadn't muddied Foxy. How could he have been muddying dogs when he was judging? He had the means, and maybe a motive, but he had had no opportunity. That meant Judge "Biscuits" Gibbs was not the Phantom Mudder.

Who else would want to spoil the show?

Judge Gibbs, the dogs, and the

people showing dogs were all eliminated as suspects. That left people *not* showing dogs!

How about Muddy Boots? He liked to wear mud on his boots. Sarge had said he couldn't show his biting poodle. Muddy Boots had been angry about that.

Was Muddy Boots still at the dog show? I set out to investigate.

<u>Jack's Glossary</u>

Bathwater. *One of the worst words I know.*

Foxed. *Fooled by a fox terrier.*

Paw-rensic testing. *Testing done by squashing evidence with the paw.*

Paw thing. *Up on hind legs, paws held together as if praying. Means happy excitement.*

Jaw-rensic testing. *Testing done by chewing evidence.*

 *Jack Undercover*

I found Muddy Boots with Mr. Latiman. The chihuahuas sat beside them.

Sniff-sniffing gave me a good whiff of Muddy Boots's boots. The boots still had gray mud on them. The mud on the muddied dogs had been *black* mud.

So Muddy Boots was not the Phantom Mudder. The mud color was all wrong. "You're slack, Jack," I said. "You should have thought of that."

"Only a slack Jack would come

near *us*," said one of the chihuahuas. He showed all his teeth. "I see a terrier toothpick."

"*I* see a classless chihuahua," I said. I Jack-jumped out of the way. I didn't want to be forced to hurt the chihuahua.

I didn't wait around to investigate Mr. Latiman. The Phantom Mudder had dog biscuits. If Mr. Latiman had dog biscuits, the chihuahuas would have swallowed them long ago.

I wasn't afraid of chihuahuas, of course. Any Jack is worth a dozen chihuahuas, and there were only three. All the same, I hurried back to Auntie Tidge, who was sitting with Dora Barkins and the squekes.

I settled down and chewed my **squeaker bone.** It was lucky that Auntie

Tidge had brought it. I do my best
thinking when I'm exercising my jaws.

As I chewed, Lord Red trotted up
with Caterina Smith on the other end of
a leash. Red was damp around the ears,
but he looked quite cheerful.

Caterina Smith smiled at Auntie
Tidge and Dora. "Are you enjoying the
show?"

"Of course, dear," said Auntie Tidge.
"Hello, Lordie."

Lord Red greeted Auntie Tidge. He
put his paws around her neck and
slurped his tongue up her cheek.

"Lordie, *no!*" snapped Caterina
Smith. "I'm sorry," she said to Auntie
Tidge.

Auntie Tidge hugged Red, then dried
her face with her scarf. "I love dogs, and

I'm used to Foxy Woxy and Jackie Wackie greeting me."

Foxy jumped up and greeted Auntie Tidge.

Caterina Smith sighed. "Lordie greeted Mrs. Gibbs this morning. That woman *does* seem to have bad luck at shows. She's had her shoes chewed, and her lipstick swallowed, and goodness knows what else. I wonder why she ever married a dog show judge if she doesn't like dogs."

"Judge Gibbs has only been judging dog shows for a couple of years," said Dora Barkins. "He used to judge cat shows."

"I'd better get Lordie dry before the big-dog class," said Caterina Smith. "Which class is next, Dora?"

Dora Barkins looked at her dog

show schedule. "It's the shih tzu class next, and then small dogs."

Before they left, Lord Red put his nose down near mine. "You will catch the Phantom Mudder, Jack," said Red. "I know you will."

The loudhowler howled, "Shih tzu class!"

The Doggeroo Dog Show was almost over, and I still had the Mudder to catch.

I had been at the end of my leash, but now I had a new lead.

It was time for Jack Russell to go undercover as a show dog.

I chewed open a box of Pooch Polish and rolled in it. I sneezed as I cleaned every toe.

I raced around the hall, giving

simple instructions to all the small dogs.
I instructed Polly, Jill Russell, the
squekes, and Shuffle the pug. I
instructed every small dog I could find.

"Beg for attention. Pretend to be
cold. Pretend to be frightened. Quiver
and quake. Shiver and shake. Yip a lot.
Do whatever it takes."

Did they do as they were told? Of
course they did! How could they disobey
a Jack on a mission?

Within minutes, half the people in
the Doggeroo Dog Show were cuddling

quivering, quaking, yipping, shivering, shaking small dogs.

"What's wrong with them?" Dora Barkins wailed as the squekes quivered and quaked.

"Don't worry, dear," said Auntie Tidge. "I expect they're just—"

I'm not sure what Auntie Tidge was planning to say, because Foxy jumped into her arms. It must have been his own idea. I hadn't instructed *him*.

It was time to bait the trap. The shih tzu class would soon be over, so I had only a few minutes to get myself doggled and muddied.

I set off in search of the Phantom Mudder of Doggeroo.

Jack's Glossary

Squeaker bone. *Item for exercising teeth. Not to be confused with a toy.*

Splat

I was sure I had now identified the Phantom Mudder, but I had to prove it. I had to catch the Mudder in the act. And that meant getting muddied.

I trotted about the hall, looking as elegant as I could.

Come on, Mudder, I thought. *You're not going to pass up a chance to muddy the only available small dog?*

I trotted past Muddy Boots and Mr. Latiman. The poodle and the chihuahuas sneered at me. I trotted past Shuffle the pug, snug in his person's arms. I trotted past Caterina

Smith and Lord Red. And then I trotted past Sarge.

"Jack. Where are you going?" asked Sarge. "You come back here!"

I trotted past High Heels, the woman Red had greeted. I trotted past Gloria Smote, who was cuddling Polly.

Then I trotted back the way I had come.

I had passed Gloria Smote and Polly when my super-sniffer detected soap and a hint of dog biscuit. Some dogs might have missed it, but you can't fool a tracking Jack with a superior super-sniffer. I spun around and sniffed.

There were two tiny biscuits lying on the ground.

I snapped one up and subjected it to jaw-rensic testing. By the time I had tested the second one, a third one had appeared. Soon there was a fourth.

I ate my way along a trail of biscuits
and hid behind a bale of hay. I was
really getting into this undercover work.

Splat.

Suddenly, I was undercover all
right—undercover of a bucket of mud.

"Got you, dog!" The Phantom
Mudder said it softly, but *nothing* has

better ears than a Jack, even when the Jack is crunching dog biscuits and has mud in his ears.

"No," I yapped, "I got *you!*" I let fly with the famous **Jack-yap**. And then I Jack-jumped right into the arms of . . .

Jack's Glossary

Jack-yap. *An especially piercing yap made by a Jack Russell.*

The Phantom
Mudder Revealed

. . . the Phantom Mudder.

Between Jack-yaps, I greeted her several times.

I beat my tail. I flung my paws around her. Then I slurped her cheek.

She tried to drop me, but I Jack-jumped up again and clung with my paws in her pockets.

Sarge heard my Jack-yap and ran to give me backup. After him came Foxy and Auntie Tidge, Red and Caterina Smith, and Judge Gibbs.

After *them* came Polly and the squekes, Gloria Smote, Dora Barkins,

Jill Russell, Shuffle, and everyone else.

"What's going on?" asked Sarge sternly. (Sarge is good at being stern.)

Judge Gibbs stared at High Heels. "Kate! What's happened?"

"This *dog* has put mud all over me!" snarled High Heels. (That's right. The Phantom Mudder was Judge Gibbs's wife.)

"She muddied me first," I Jack-yapped. "There is no doubt in my mind that she is the Phantom Mudder."

Sarge cleared his throat. "Mrs. Gibbs, is that your bucket?" He pointed to the muddy bucket the Mudder had dropped when I Jack-jumped up to greet her.

"No, it's mine," said Judge Gibbs. "Kate, what have you *done*?"

Mrs. Gibbs stamped her foot,

splashing mud over Sarge, Auntie Tidge, and Caterina Smith. "It's not fair!" she said. "I hate dog shows. I've had my shoes ruined and my fingers bitten. I had my gold lipstick eaten by a bulldog. Today was the last straw." She pointed to Red. "That setter spoiled my new coat with mud, so I thought I'd spoil a few dog coats in revenge."

"But Kate, what did you hope to achieve?" asked Judge Gibbs.

"I wanted to stop the show," said Kate Gibbs in a sulky voice. "Give me a cat show any day! *Cats* don't chew my shoes and eat my lipsticks and wipe mud all over my coat." She glared at Sarge. "But you didn't stop the show, did you? You just moved the muddy dogs into other classes!"

That's how Jack Russell, Dog Detective, solved the case of the Phantom Mudder. My superior super-sniffer wasn't at its best that day, so I had to rely on other methods of detection.

1. I eliminated suspects like dogs, their people, Judge Gibbs, Mr. Latiman, and Muddy Boots.

2. I took the suspect's motive into account. She'd told Caterina Smith how lots of dogs had bothered her at shows. Mr. Latiman said Muddy Boots's dog had bitten the judge's wife the year before.

3. I took means and opportunity and evidence into account. High Heels could have gotten dog biscuits from Judge Gibbs. She had a show schedule, so she'd known just which dogs to muddy before their classes. She always smelled of soap because she washed her hands every time she muddied a dog.

4. I took character into account. High Heels stepped on Red's tail. Then she almost stepped on Foxy and me.

That's right.

You guessed it.

I got another bath.

Jack's Glossary

Unspecial biscuit. *The kind of biscuit people eat.*

5. Finally, she called me a *sweet little doggie*. No innocent person would insult a Jack like that.

What happened afterward?

The show went on, of course. Polly won the small-dog class. Red won the big-dog class.

Auntie Tidge got the Phantom Mudder a cup of tea and an **unspecial biscuit.**

Sarge banned the Phantom Mudder from ever going to dog shows. He said she should go to cat shows instead.

Auntie Tidge gave Foxy and me special biscuits.

And what was my reward for solving the case of the Phantom Mudder?

Impreso y encuadernado en GRAFICA GUADALUPE
Av. San Martín 3773 (1847) Rafael Calzada
en el mes de **marzo de 1996**